The Junior Great Books Reading and Discussion Program

JUNIOR GREAT BOOKS

Series Five
First Semester, Volume One

A Program of Interpretive Reading and Discussion

The Great Books Foundation
a nonprofit educational corporation

Published and distributed by
The Great Books Foundation
a nonprofit educational corporation
40 East Huron Street
Chicago, Illinois 60611

Acknowledgments

All possible care has been taken to trace ownership and secure permission for each selection included in this series. The Great Books Foundation acknowledges with gratitude its indebtedness to the following authors, publishers, and representatives for permission to include the following copyright material:

Charles from THE LOTTERY AND OTHER STORIES by Shirley Jackson. Copyright © 1948, 1949 by Shirley Jackson, renewed 1976, 1977 by Laurence Hyman, Barry Hyman, Mrs. Sarah Webster, and Mrs. Joanne Schnurer. Reprinted by permission of Farrar, Straus and Giroux, Inc.

The Nightingale from HANS CHRISTIAN ANDERSEN: THE COMPLETE FAIRY TALES AND STORIES translated by Erik Christian Haugaard. Translation copyright © 1974 by Erik Christian Haugaard. Reprinted by permission of Doubleday & Company, Inc.

Thank You, M'am from THE LANGSTON HUGHES READER by Langston Hughes. Copyright © 1958 by Langston Hughes. Reprinted by permission of Harold Ober Associates, Incorporated.

The King and the Shirt and *The Two Brothers* from FABLES AND FAIRY TALES by Leo Tolstoy, translated by Ann Dunnigan. Copyright © 1962 by Ann Dunnigan. Reprinted by arrangement with The New American Library, Inc.

Fresh from WHAT THE NEIGHBOURS DID AND OTHER STORIES by Philippa Pearce. Copyright © 1959, 1967, 1969, 1972 by Philippa Pearce. By permission of Harper & Row, Publishers, Inc.

Echo and Narcissus from THE FABER BOOK OF GREEK LEGENDS edited by Kathleen Lines. Published by Faber & Faber, Ltd.

All Summer in a Day by Ray Bradbury. Copyright © 1954 by Ray Bradbury, renewed 1982 by Ray Bradbury. Reprinted by permission of the Harold Matson Company, Inc.

Kaddo's Wall from THE COW-TAIL SWITCH AND OTHER WEST AFRICAN STORIES by Harold Courlander and George Herzog. Copyright © 1947, 1975 by Harold Courlander and George Herzog. By permission of Harold Courlander.

The Fifty-First Dragon from SEEING THINGS AT NIGHT by Heywood Broun. Copyright © 1921 by Heywood Broun, renewed 1941 by Heywood Hale Broun. By permission of Bill Cooper Associates, Inc.

Spit Nolan from THE GOALKEEPER'S REVENGE by Bill Naughton. Copyright by Bill Naughton. By permission of A. D. Peters & Co., Writers' Agents.

Maurice's Room from MAURICE'S ROOM by Paula Fox. Copyright © 1966 by Paula Fox. Reprinted with permission of Macmillan Publishing Co., Inc.

Ed Young prepared the illustrations for this series.

Cover illustrations by Ed Young and Donna Diamond.

Cover and book design by Michael Waitsman and Liane Sebastian, Synthesis Concepts, Inc.

Contents

Charles

Shirley Jackson

The day my son Laurie started kindergarten he renounced corduroy overalls with bibs and began wearing blue jeans with a belt; I watched him go off the first morning with the older girl next door, seeing clearly that an era of my life was ended, my sweet-voiced nursery-school tot replaced by a long-trousered, swaggering character who forgot to stop at the corner and wave good-bye to me.

He came home the same way, the front door slamming open, his cap on the floor, and the voice suddenly become raucous shouting, "Isn't anybody *here?*"

At lunch he spoke insolently to his father, spilled his baby sister's milk, and remarked that his teacher said we were not to take the name of the Lord in vain.

"How *was* school today?" I asked, elaborately casual.

"All right," he said.

"Did you learn anything?" his father asked.

Laurie regarded his father coldly. "I didn't learn nothing," he said.

"Anything," I said. "Didn't learn anything."

"The teacher spanked a boy, though," Laurie said, addressing his bread and butter. "For being fresh," he added, with his mouth full.

"What did he do?" I asked. "Who was it?"

Laurie thought. "It was Charles," he said. "He was fresh. The teacher spanked him and made him stand in a corner. He was awfully fresh."

"What did he do?" I asked again, but Laurie slid off his chair, took a cookie, and left, while his father was still saying, "See here, young man."

The next day Laurie remarked at lunch, as soon as he sat down, "Well, Charles was bad again today." He grinned enormously and said, "Today Charles hit the teacher."

"Good heavens," I said, mindful of the Lord's name, "I suppose he got spanked again?"

"He sure did," Laurie said. "Look up," he said to his father.

"What?" his father said, looking up.

"Look down," Laurie said. "Look at my thumb. Gee, you're dumb." He began to laugh insanely.

"Why did Charles hit the teacher?" I asked quickly.

"Because she tried to make him color with red crayons," Laurie said. "Charles wanted to color with green crayons so he hit the teacher and she spanked him and said nobody play with Charles but everbody did."

The third day—it was Wednesday of the first week—Charles bounced a see-saw on to the head of a little girl and made her bleed, and the teacher made him stay inside all during recess. Thursday Charles had to stand in a corner during story-time because he kept pounding his feet on the floor. Friday Charles was deprived of blackboard privileges because he threw chalk.

On Saturday I remarked to my husband, "Do you think kindergarten is too unsettling for Laurie? All this toughness, and bad grammar, and this Charles boy sounds like such a bad influence."

"It'll be all right," my husband said reassuringly. "Bound to be people like Charles in the world. Might as well meet them now as later."

On Monday Laurie came home late, full of news. "Charles," he shouted as he came up the hill; I was waiting anxiously on the front steps. "Charles," Laurie yelled all the way up the hill, "Charles was bad again."

"Come right in," I said, as soon as he came close enough. "Lunch is waiting."

"You know what Charles did?" he demanded, following me through the door. "Charles yelled so in school they sent a boy in from first grade to tell the teacher she had to make Charles keep quiet, and so Charles had to stay after school. And so all the children stayed to watch him."

"What did he do?" I asked.

"He just sat there," Laurie said, climbing into his chair at the table. "Hi, Pop, y'old dust mop."

"Charles had to stay after school today," I told my husband. "Everyone stayed with him."

"What does this Charles look like?" my husband asked Laurie. "What's his other name?"

"He's bigger than me," Laurie said. "And he doesn't have any rubbers and he doesn't ever wear a jacket."

Monday night was the first Parent-Teachers meeting, and only the fact that the baby had a cold kept me from going; I wanted passionately to meet Charles's mother. On Tuesday Laurie remarked suddenly, "Our teacher had a friend come to see her in school today."

"Charles's mother?" my husband and I asked simultaneously.

"Naaah," Laurie said scornfully. "It was a man who came and made us do exercises, we had to touch our toes. Look." He climbed down from his chair and squatted down and touched his toes. "Like this," he said. He got solemnly back into his chair and said, picking up his fork, "Charles didn't even *do* exercises."

"That's fine," I said heartily. "Didn't Charles want to do exercises?"

"Naaah," Laurie said. "Charles was so fresh to the teacher's friend he wasn't *let* do exercises."

"Fresh again?" I said.

"He kicked the teacher's friend," Laurie said. "The teacher's friend told Charles to touch his toes like I just did and Charles kicked him."

"What are they going to do about Charles, do you suppose?" Laurie's father asked him.

Laurie shrugged elaborately. "Throw him out of school, I guess," he said.

Wednesday and Thursday were routine; Charles yelled during story hour and hit a boy in the stomach and made him cry. On Friday Charles stayed after school again and so did all the other children.

With the third week of kindergarten Charles was an institution in our family; the baby was being a Charles when she cried all afternoon; Laurie did a Charles when he filled his wagon full of mud and pulled it through the kitchen; even my husband, when he caught his elbow in the telephone cord and pulled telephone, ashtray, and a bowl of flowers off the table, said, after the first minute, "Looks like Charles."

During the third and fourth weeks it looked like a reformation in Charles; Laurie reported grimly at lunch on Thursday of the third week, "Charles was so good today the teacher gave him an apple."

"What?" I said, and my husband added warily, "You mean Charles?"

"Charles," Laurie said. "He gave the crayons around and he picked up the books afterward and the teacher said he was her helper."

"What happened?" I asked incredulously.

"He was her helper, that's all," Laurie said, and shrugged.

"Can this be true, about Charles?" I asked my husband that night. "Can something like this happen?"

"Wait and see," my husband said cynically. "When

you've got a Charles to deal with, this may mean he's only plotting."

He seemed to be wrong. For over a week Charles was the teacher's helper; each day he handed things out and he picked things up; no one had to stay after school.

"The P.T.A. meeting's next week again," I told my husband one evening. "I'm going to find Charles's mother there."

"Ask her what happened to Charles," my husband said. "I'd like to know."

"I'd like to know myself," I said.

On Friday of that week things were back to normal. "You know what Charles did today?" Laurie demanded at the lunch table, in a voice slightly awed. "He told a little girl to say a word and she said it and the teacher washed her mouth out with soap and Charles laughed."

"What word?" his father asked unwisely, and Laurie said, "I'll have to whisper it to you, it's so bad." He got down off his chair and went around to his father. His father bent his head down and Laurie whispered joyfully. His father's eyes widened.

"Did Charles tell the little girl to say *that?*" he asked respectfully.

"She said it *twice,*" Laurie said. "Charles told her to say it *twice.*"

"What happened to Charles?" my husband asked.

"Nothing," Laurie said. "He was passing out the crayons."

Monday morning Charles abandoned the little girl and

said the evil word himself three or four times, getting his mouth washed out with soap each time. He also threw chalk.

My husband came to the door with me that evening as I set out for the P.T.A. meeting. "Invite her over for a cup of tea after the meeting," he said. "I want to get a look at her."

"If only she's there," I said prayerfully.

"She'll be there," my husband said. "I don't see how they could hold a P.T.A. meeting without Charles's mother."

At the meeting I sat restlessly, scanning each comfortable matronly face, trying to determine which one hid the secret of Charles. None of them looked to me haggard enough. No one stood up in the meeting and apologized for the way her son had been acting. No one mentioned Charles.

After the meeting I identified and sought out Laurie's kindergarten teacher. She had a plate with a cup of tea and a piece of chocolate cake; I had a plate with a cup of tea and a piece of marshmallow cake. We maneuvered up to one another cautiously and smiled.

"I've been so anxious to meet you," I said. "I'm Laurie's mother."

"We're all so interested in Laurie," she said.

"Well, he certainly likes kindergarten," I said. "He talks about it all the time."

"We had a little trouble adjusting, the first week or so," she said primly, "but now he's a fine little helper. With occasional lapses, of course."

"Laurie usually adjusts very quickly," I said. "I suppose this time it's Charles's influence."

"Charles?"

"Yes," I said, laughing, "you must have your hands full in that kindergarten, with Charles."

"Charles?" she said. "We don't have any Charles in the kindergarten."

Interpretive Questions

1. Why does Laurie invent Charles?
2. Why are Laurie's parents more interested in Charles' behavior in kindergarten than they are in their son's?
3. Why does Laurie have Charles become the teacher's helper in the third week of school?

Shared Inquiry

In a Junior Great Books discussion you will search for a story's meaning. The search may center on the story as a whole, on particular passages, or even on a few words. It doesn't matter how much or how little of the story you are thinking about, as long as the process helps you discover what the author wants to tell you or make you feel through his words.

The leader's job is to help you think for yourself about what a story means. Leaders always start a discussion with an interpretive question they are not sure how to answer. Sometimes this is because they think a question can be answered correctly in more than one way. Sometimes they may not have found any answer that satisfies them. In either case, leaders will share real questions about meaning with you and ask for your help in answering them. For this reason, the method of discussion is called *shared inquiry.*

One of the pleasures of shared inquiry is that you are free to give the best answer you can think of without worrying about whether it is "the" right answer—many times there will be more than one right answer. You are equally free not to answer at all if you have nothing to say at the moment. If you do answer a question, a leader may ask you what in the story makes you think your answer is correct. Other students are free to agree or disagree with you but they, too, will be asked to back up their answers with facts from the story. As a result of what you hear, you may change your mind about your answer. Shared inquiry gives you the chance to learn from the author and from one another.

By the end of a good discussion you will understand the story better than you did before exchanging ideas. People will not always agree on a single interpretation, but that's part of what makes it interesting and fun to discuss the stories in Junior Great Books. ■

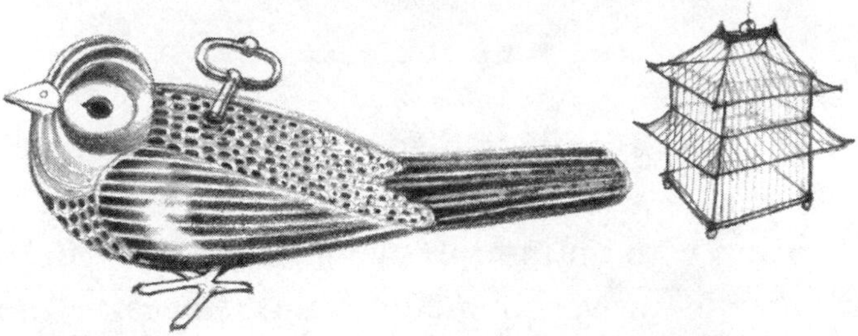

The Nightingale

Hans Christian Andersen

In China, as you know, the emperor is Chinese, and so are his court and all his people. This story happened a long, long time ago; and that is just the reason why you should hear it now, before it is forgotten. The emperor's palace was the most beautiful in the whole world. It was made of porcelain and had been most costly to build. It was so fragile that you had to be careful not to touch anything, and that can be difficult. The gardens were filled with the loveliest flowers; the most beautiful of them had little silver bells that tinkled so you wouldn't pass by without noticing them.

Everything in the emperor's garden was most cunningly arranged. The gardens were so large that even the head gardener did not know exactly how big they were. If you kept walking you finally came to the most beautiful forest with tall trees that mirrored themselves in deep lakes.

The forest stretched all the way to the sea, which was blue and so deep that even large boats could sail so close to the shore that they were shaded by the trees. Here lived a nightingale who sang so sweetly that even the fisherman, who came every night to set his nets, would stop to rest when he heard it and say: "Blessed God, how beautifully it sings!" But he couldn't listen too long, for he had work to do, and soon he would forget the bird. Yet the next night when he heard it again, he would repeat what he had said the night before: "Blessed God, how beautifully it sings!"

From all over the world travelers came to the emperor's city to admire his palace and gardens; but when they heard the nightingale sing, they all declared that it was the loveliest of all. When they returned to their own countries, they would write long and learned books about the city, the palace, and the garden; but they didn't forget the nightingale. No, that was always mentioned in the very first chapter. Those who could write poetry wrote long odes about the nightingale who lived in the forest, on the shores of the deep blue sea.

These books were read the whole world over; and finally one was also sent to the emperor. He sat down in his golden chair and started to read it. Every once in a while he would nod his head because it pleased him to read how his own city and his own palace and gardens were praised; but then he came to the sentence "But the song of the nightingale is the loveliest of all."

"What!" said the emperor. "The nightingale? I don't know it, I have never heard of it; and yet it lives not only in my empire but in my very garden. That is the sort of thing one can only find out by reading books."

He called his chief courtier, who was so very noble that if anyone of a rank lower than his own either talked to him or dared ask him a question, he only answered "P." And that didn't mean anything at all.

"There is a strange and famous bird called the nightingale," began the emperor. "It is thought to be the most marvelous thing in my empire. Why have I never heard of it?"

"I have never heard of it," answered the courtier. "It has never been presented at court."

"I want it to come this evening and sing for me," demanded the emperor. "The whole world knows of it, but I do not."

"I have never heard it mentioned before," said the courtier, and bowed. "But I shall search for it and find it."

But that was more easily said than done. The courtier ran all through the palace, up the stairs and down the stairs, and through the long corridors, but none of the people whom he asked had ever heard of the nightingale. He returned to the emperor and declared that the whole story was nothing but a fable, invented by those people who had written the books. "Your Imperial Majesty should not believe everything that is written. A discovery is one thing and artistic imagination something quite different; it is fiction."

"The book I have just read," replied the emperor, "was sent to me by the great Emperor of Japan; and therefore, every word in it must be the truth. I want to hear the nightingale! And that tonight! If it does not come, then the whole court shall have their stomachs thumped, and that right after they have eaten."

"Tsing-pe!" said the courtier. He ran again up and down the stairs and through the corridors; and half the court ran with him, because they didn't want their stomachs thumped! Everywhere they asked about the nightingale that the whole world knew about, and yet no one at court had heard of.

At last they came to the kitchen, where a poor little girl worked, scrubbing the pots and pans. "Oh, I know the nightingale," she said. "I know it well, it sings so beautifully. Every evening I am allowed to bring some leftovers to my poor sick mother who lives down by the sea. Now it is far away, and as I return I often rest in the forest and listen to the nightingale. I get tears in my eyes from it, as though my mother were kissing me."

"Little kitchenmaid," said the courtier, "I will arrange for a permanent position in the kitchen for you, and permission to see the emperor eat, if you will take us to the nightingale; it is summoned to court tonight."

Half the court went to the forest to find the nightingale. As they were walking along, a cow began to bellow.

"Oh!" shouted all the courtiers. "There it is. What a marvelously powerful voice the little animal has; we have heard it before."

"That is only a cow," said the little kitchenmaid. "We are still far from where the nightingale lives."

They passed a little pond; the frogs were croaking.

"Lovely," sighed the Chinese imperial dean. "I can

hear her, she sounds like little church bells ringing."

"No, that is only the frogs," said the little kitchenmaid, "but any time now we may hear it."

Just then the nightingale began singing.

"There it is!" said the little girl. "Listen. Listen. It is up there on that branch." And she pointed to a little gray bird sitting amid the greenery.

"Is that possible?" exclaimed the chief courtier. "I had not imagined it would look like that. It looks so common! I think it has lost its color from shyness and out of embarrassment at seeing so many noble people at one time."

"Little nightingale," called the kitchenmaid, "our emperor wants you to sing for him."

"With pleasure," replied the nightingale, and sang as beautifully as he could.

"It sounds like little glass bells," sighed the chief courtier. "Look at its little throat, how it throbs. It is strange that we have never heard of it before; it will be a great success at court."

"Shall I sing another song for the emperor?" asked the nightingale, who thought that the emperor was there.

"Most excellent little nightingale," began the chief courtier, "I have the pleasure to invite you to attend the court tonight, where His Imperial Majesty, The Emperor of China, wishes you to enchant him with your most charming art."

"It sounds best in the green woods," said the nightingale; but when he heard that the emperor insisted, he followed them readily back to the palace.

There every room had been polished and thousands of

little golden lamps reflected themselves in the shiny porcelain walls and floors. In the corridors stood all the most beautiful flowers, the ones with silver bells on them; and there was such a draft from all the servants running in and out, and opening and closing doors, that all the bells were tinkling and you couldn't hear what anyone said.

In the grand banquet hall, where the emperor's throne stood, a little golden perch had been hung for the nightingale to sit on. The whole court was there, and the little kitchenmaid, who now had the title of Imperial Kitchenmaid, was allowed to stand behind one of the doors and listen. Everyone was dressed in their finest clothes, and they were all looking at the little gray bird, towards which the emperor nodded very kindly.

The nightingale's song was so sweet that tears came into the emperor's eyes; and when they ran down his cheeks, the little nightingale sang even more beautifully than it had before. His song spoke to one's heart, and the emperor was so pleased that he ordered his golden slipper to be hung around the little bird's neck. There was no higher honor. But the nightingale thanked him and said that he had been honored enough already.

"I have seen tears in the eyes of an emperor, and that is a great enough treasure for me. There is a strange power in an emperor's tears, and God knows that is reward enough." Then he sang yet another song.

"That was the most charming and elegant song we have ever heard," said all the ladies of the court. And from that time onward they filled their mouths with water so they could make a clucking noise whenever anyone spoke to them, because they thought that then they sounded like the nightingale. Even the chambermaids and the lackeys were satisfied; and that really meant something, for servants are the most difficult to please. Yes, the nightingale was a success.

He was to have his own cage at court, and permission to take a walk twice a day and once during the night. Twelve servants were to accompany him; each held on tightly to a silk ribbon that was attached to the poor bird's legs. There wasn't any pleasure in such an outing.

The whole town talked about the marvelous bird. Whenever two people met in the street, they would sigh; one would say "night" and the other "gale"; and then they would understand each other perfectly. Twelve delicatessen shop owners named their children "Nightingale," but not one of them could sing.

One day a package arrived for the emperor; on it was written "Nightingale."

"It is probably another book about our famous bird," said the emperor. But he was wrong; it was a mechanical nightingale. It lay in a little box and was supposed to look like the real one, though it was made of silver and gold and studded with sapphires, diamonds, and rubies. When you wound it up, it could sing one of the songs the real nightingale sang; and while it performed, its little silver tail would go up and down. Around its neck hung a ribbon on which was written: "The Emperor of Japan's nightingale is inferior to the Emperor of China's."

"It is beautiful!" exclaimed the whole court. And the messenger who brought it had the title of Supreme Imperial Nightingale Deliverer bestowed upon him at once.

"They ought to sing together, it will be a duet," said everyone. And they did. But that didn't work out well at all, for the real bird sang in his own manner and the mechanical one had a cylinder inside its chest instead of a heart. "It is not its fault," said the imperial music master. "It keeps perfect time. It belongs to my school of music." Then the mechanical nightingale had to sing solo. Everyone agreed that its song was just as beautiful as the real nightingale's; and besides, the artificial bird was much pleasanter to look at, with its sapphires, rubies, and diamonds that glittered like bracelets and brooches.

The mechanical nightingale sang its song thirty-three times and did not grow tired. The court would have liked to hear it the thirty-fourth time, but the emperor thought that the real nightingale ought to sing now. But where was it? Nobody had noticed that he had flown out through an open window to his beloved green forest.

"What is the meaning of this!" said the emperor angrily, and the whole court blamed the nightingale and called him an ungrateful creature.

"But the best bird remains," they said, and the mechanical bird sang its song once more. It was the same song, for it knew no other; but it was very intricate, so the courtiers didn't know it by heart yet. The imperial music master praised the bird and declared that it was better than the real nightingale, not only on the outside where the diamonds were, but also inside.

"Your Imperial Majesty and gentlemen: you understand that the real nightingale cannot be depended upon.

One never knows what he will sing, whereas in the mechanical bird everything is determined. There is one song and no other! One can explain everything. We can open it up to examine and appreciate how human thought has fashioned the wheels and the cylinder and put them where they are, to turn just as they should."

"Precisely what I was thinking!" said the whole court in a chorus. And the imperial music master was given permission to show the new nightingale to the people on the following Sunday.

The emperor thought that they, too, should hear the bird. They did, and they were as delighted as if they had got drunk on too much tea. It was all very Chinese. They pointed with their licking fingers toward heaven, nodded, and said "Oh!"

But the poor fisherman, who had heard the real nightingale, mumbled, "It sounds beautiful and like the bird's song, but something is missing, though I don't know what it is."

The real nightingale was banished from the empire.

The mechanical bird was given a silk pillow to rest upon, close to the emperor's bed; and all the presents it had received were piled around it. Among them were both gold and precious stones. Its title was Supreme Imperial Night-table Singer and its rank was Number One to the Left—the emperor thought the left side was more distinguished because that is the side where the heart is, even in an emperor.

The imperial music master wrote a work in twenty-five volumes about the mechanical nightingale. It was not only long and learned, but filled with the most difficult Chinese words, so everyone bought it and said they had read and understood it, for otherwise they would have been considered stupid and had to have their stomachs poked.

A whole year went by. The emperor, the court, and all the Chinese in China knew every note of the Supreme Imperial Night-table Singer's song by heart. But that was the very reason why they liked it so much; they could sing it themselves, and they did. The street urchins sang "Zi-zi-zizzi, cluck-cluck-cluck-cluck." And so did the emperor. Oh, it was delightful.

But one evening, when the bird was singing its very best and the emperor was lying in bed listening to it, something said "Clang" inside it. It was broken! All the wheels whirred around, and then the bird was still.

The emperor jumped out of bed and called his physician, but he couldn't do anything. So the imperial watchmaker was fetched. After a great deal of talking and tinkering he repaired the bird, but he declared that the cylinders were worn and new ones could not be fitted. The bird would have to be spared; it could not be played so often.

It was a catastrophe. Only once a year was the mechanical bird allowed to sing, and then it had difficulty finishing its song. But the imperial music master made a speech wherein he explained, using the most difficult words, that the bird was as good as ever. And then it was.

Five years passed, and a great misfortune happened. Although everyone loved the old emperor, he had fallen ill; and they all agreed that he would not get well again. It was said that a new emperor had already been chosen; and when people in the street asked the chief courtier how the emperor was, he would shake his head and say "P."

Pale and cold, the emperor lay in his golden bed. The whole court believed him to be already dead, and they were busy visiting and paying their respects to the new emperor. The lackeys were all out in the street gossiping, and the chambermaids were drinking coffee. All the floors in the whole palace were covered with black carpets so that no one's steps would disturb the dying emperor, and that's why it was as quiet as quiet could be in the whole palace.

But the emperor was not dead yet. Pale and motionless, he lay in his great golden bed. The long velvet curtains were drawn, and the golden tassels moved slowly in the wind, for one of the windows was open. The moon shone down upon the emperor, and its light was reflected in the diamonds of the mechanical bird.

The emperor could hardly breathe; he felt as though someone were sitting on his chest. He opened his eyes. Death was sitting there. He was wearing the emperor's golden crown and held his gold sabre in one hand and his imperial banner in the other. From the folds of the curtains that hung around his bed, strange faces looked down at the emperor. Some of them were frighteningly ugly, and others mild and kind. They were the evil and good deeds that the emperor had done. Now, while Death was sitting on his heart, they were looking down at him.

"Do you remember?" whispered first one and then another. And they told him things that made the cold sweat of fear appear on his forehead.

"No, no, I don't remember! It is not true!" shouted the emperor. "Music, music, play the great Chinese gong," he begged, "so that I will not be able to hear what they are saying."

But the faces kept talking and Death, like a real Chinese, nodded his head to every word that was said.

"Little golden nightingale, sing!" demanded the emperor. "I have given you gold and precious jewels, and with my own hands have I hung my golden slipper around your neck. Sing! Please sing!"

But the mechanical nightingale stood as still as ever, for there was no one to wind it up; and then, it couldn't sing.

Death kept staring at the emperor out of the empty sockets in his skull; and the palace was still, so terrifyingly still.

All at once the most beautiful song broke the silence. It was the nightingale, who had heard of the emperor's illness and torment. He sat on a branch outside his window and sang to bring him comfort and hope. As he sang, the faces in the folds of the curtains faded, and the blood pulsed with greater force through the emperor's weak body. Death himself listened and said, "Please, little nightingale, sing on!"

"Will you give me the golden sabre? Will you give me the imperial banner? Will you give me the golden crown?"

Death gave each of his trophies for a song; and then

the nightingale sang about the quiet churchyard, where white roses grow, where fragrant elderberry trees are, and where the grass is green from the tears of those who come to mourn. Death longed so much for his garden that he flew out of the window, like a white cold mist.

"Thank you, thank you," whispered the emperor, "you heavenly little bird, I remember you. You have I banished from my empire, and yet you came to sing for me; and when you sang, the evil phantoms that taunted me disappeared, and Death himself left my heart. How shall I reward you?"

"You have rewarded me already," said the nightingale. "I shall never forget that the first time I sang for you, you gave me the tears from your eyes; and to a poet's heart, those are jewels. But sleep so you can become well and strong; I shall sing for you."

The little gray bird sang; and the emperor slept, so blessedly, so peacefully.

The sun was shining in through the window when he woke; he did not feel ill any more. None of his servants had come, for they thought that he was already dead; but the nightingale was still there, and he was singing.

"You must come always," declared the emperor. "I shall only ask you to sing when you want to. And the mechanical bird I shall break in a thousand pieces."

"Don't do that," replied the nightingale. "The mechanical bird sang as well as it could. Keep it. I can't build my nest in the palace; let me come to visit you when I want to, and I shall sit on the branch outside your window and sing for you. And my song shall make you happy and make you thoughtful. I shall sing not only of those who are happy, but also of those who suffer. I shall sing of the good and of the evil that happen around you and yet are hidden from you. For a little songbird flies far. I visit the poor fisherman's cottage and the peasant's hut, far away from your palace and your court. I love your heart more than your crown, and yet I feel that the crown has a fragrance of something holy about it. I will come! I will sing for you! Only one thing you must promise me."

"I will promise you anything," said the emperor, who had dressed himself in his imperial clothes and was holding his golden sabre, pressing it against his heart.

"I beg of you, never tell anyone that you have a little bird that tells you everything, for then you will fare even better." And with those words the nightingale flew away.

The servants entered the room to look at their dead master. There they stood gaping when the emperor said: "Good morning."

Interpretive Questions

1. Which is more dependable—a real nightingale or a mechanical one?

2. Why does the nightingale defend the mechanical bird, saying that it sang as well as it could?

3. In the story, what does it mean to have a heart?

What We Mean by Interpretation

Good writers, like all good craftsmen, do their work with care. They have reasons for everything they put into their stories. They try to include only what has a point and what fits—the things needed to make a story clear, to make it interesting, and to keep it moving along. They waste few words. In really good stories, everything fits and everything has an explanation. The parts are connected and support one another just as the posts and beams in a building do.

The parts of a story, because they are connected, help to explain one another. Authors do not point out exactly how the parts are connected, nor do they explain in so many words why everything in a story happens as it does. For one thing, that would make the story dull. For another, they want stories to be convincing—to seem like real life. In our lives, few things that happen come complete with an explanation. We have to puzzle out the explanations for ourselves.

Stories, too, ask us to work out many explanations for ourselves. But reading a story is not a guessing game. Every good author puts into a story all that a reader must know to understand what is happening and why. As we figure out for ourselves the things an author includes but doesn't explain, we *interpret* what we read. To interpret a story is to explain its meaning—what happens in it, and why, and what the story is about.

Interpretation begins with questions, the questions that come to us as we read. As we work out the answers to such questions, we arrive at a clearer idea of how the parts of the story fit together and a clearer idea of its meaning—what the author wants us to think about and to experience through his words. ■

Thank You, M'am

Langston Hughes

She was a large woman with a large purse that had everything in it but a hammer and nails. It had a long strap, and she carried it slung across her shoulder. It was about eleven o'clock at night, dark, and she was walking alone, when a boy ran up behind her and tried to snatch her purse. The strap broke with the sudden single tug the boy gave it from behind. But the boy's weight and the weight of the purse combined caused him to lose his balance. Instead of taking off full blast as he had hoped, the boy fell on his back on the sidewalk and his legs flew up. The large woman simply turned around and kicked him right square in his blue-jeaned sitter. Then she reached down, picked the boy up by his shirt front, and shook him until his teeth rattled.

After that the woman said, "Pick up my pocketbook, boy, and give it here."

She still held him tightly. But she bent down enough to permit him to stoop and pick up her purse. Then she said, "Now ain't you ashamed of yourself?"

Firmly gripped by his shirt front, the boy said, "Yes'm."

The woman said, "What did you want to do it for?"

The boy said, "I didn't aim to."

She said, "You a lie!"

By that time two or three people passed, stopped, turned to look, and some stood watching.

"If I turn you loose, will you run?" asked the woman.

"Yes'm," said the boy.

"Then I won't turn you loose," said the woman. She did not release him.

"Lady, I'm sorry," whispered the boy.

"Um-hum! Your face is dirty. I got a great mind to wash your face for you. Ain't you got nobody home to tell you to wash your face?"

"No'm," said the boy.

"Then it will get washed this evening," said the large woman, starting up the street, dragging the frightened boy behind her.

He looked as if he were fourteen or fifteen, frail and willow-wild, in tennis shoes and blue jeans.

The woman said, "You ought to be my son. I would teach you right from wrong. Least I can do right now is to wash your face. Are you hungry?"

"No'm," said the being-dragged boy. "I just want you to turn me loose."

"Was I bothering *you* when I turned that corner?" asked the woman.

"No'm."

"But you put yourself in contact with *me,*" said the woman. "If you think that that contact is not going to last awhile, you got another thought coming. When I get through with you, sir, you are going to remember Mrs. Luella Bates Washington Jones."

Sweat popped out on the boy's face and he began to struggle. Mrs. Jones stopped, jerked him around in front of her, put a half nelson about his neck, and continued to drag him up the street. When she got to her door, she dragged the boy inside, down a hall, and into a large kitchenette-furnished room at the rear of the house. She switched on the light and left the door open. The boy could hear other roomers laughing and talking in the large house. Some of their doors were open, too, so he knew he and the woman were not alone. The woman still had him by the neck in the middle of her room.

She said, "What is your name?"

"Roger," answered the boy.

"Then, Roger, you go to that sink and wash your face," said the woman, whereupon she turned him loose—at last. Roger looked at the door—looked at the woman—looked at the door—*and went to the sink.*

"Let the water run until it gets warm," she said. "Here's a clean towel."

"You gonna take me to jail?" asked the boy, bending over the sink.

"Not with that face, I would not take you nowhere," said the woman. "Here I am trying to get home to cook me a bite to eat, and you snatch my pocketbook! Maybe you ain't been to your supper either, late as it be. Have you?"

"There's nobody home at my house," said the boy.

"Then we'll eat," said the woman. "I believe you're hungry—or been hungry—to try to snatch my pocketbook!"

"I want a pair of blue suede shoes," said the boy.

"Well, you didn't have to snatch *my* pocketbook to get some suede shoes," said Mrs. Luella Bates Washington Jones. "You could of asked me."

"M'am?"

The water dripping from his face, the boy looked at her. There was a long pause. A very long pause. After he had dried his face and not knowing what else to do, dried it again, the boy turned around, wondering what next. The door was open. He could make a dash for it down the hall. He could run, run, run, *run!*

The woman was sitting on the daybed. After a while she said, "I were young once and I wanted things I could not get."

There was another long pause. The boy's mouth opened. Then he frowned, not knowing he frowned.

The woman said, "Um-hum! You thought I was going to say *but,* didn't you? You thought I was going to say, *but I didn't snatch people's pocketbooks.* Well, I wasn't going to say that." Pause. Silence. "I have done things, too, which I would not tell you, son—neither tell God, if He didn't already know. Everybody's got something in common. So you set down while I fix us something to eat. You might run that comb through your hair so you will look presentable."

In another corner of the room behind a screen was a gas plate and an icebox. Mrs. Jones got up and went behind the screen. The woman did not watch the boy to see if he was going to run now, nor did she watch her purse, which she left behind her on the daybed. But the boy took care to sit on the far side of the room, away from the purse, where he thought she could easily see him out of the corner of her eye if she wanted to. He did not trust the woman *not* to trust him. And he did not want to be mistrusted now.

"Do you need somebody to go to the store," asked the boy, "maybe to get some milk or something?"

"Don't believe I do," said the woman, "unless you just want sweet milk yourself. I was going to make cocoa out of this canned milk I got here."

"That will be fine," said the boy.

She heated some lima beans and ham she had in the icebox, made the cocoa, and set the table. The woman did not ask the boy anything about where he lived, or his folks, or anything else that would embarrass him. Instead, as they ate, she told him about her job in a hotel beauty shop that stayed open late, what the work was like, and how all kinds of women came in and out, blondes, redheads, and Spanish. Then she cut him a half of her ten-cent cake.

"Eat some more, son," she said.

When they were finished eating, she got up and said, "Now here, take this ten dollars and buy yourself some blue suede shoes. And next time, do not make the mistake of latching onto *my* pocketbook *nor nobody else's*—because shoes got by devilish ways will burn your feet. I got to get my rest now. But from here on in, son, I hope you will behave yourself."

She led him down the hall to the front door and opened it. "Good night! Behave yourself, boy!" she said, looking out into the street as he went down the steps.

The boy wanted to say something other than, "Thank you, m'am," to Mrs. Luella Bates Washington Jones, but although his lips moved, he couldn't even say that as he turned at the foot of the barren stoop and looked up at the large woman in the door. Then she shut the door.

Interpretive Questions

1. Why does Mrs. Jones give Roger the money for the blue suede shoes?
2. Why do Mrs. Jones and Roger need each other?
3. Why doesn't Roger run away when Mrs. Jones turns him loose to wash his face?

Questions of Fact, Interpretation, and Evaluation

Three kinds of questions are asked in a Junior Great Books discussion: questions of fact, questions of interpretation, and questions of evaluation.

Questions of fact ask you to recall something that happened in the story. Everything the author says about the world of a story is a fact, whether or not we usually accept it as true. Knowing the facts of a story is important because we use them to support our opinions about the story's meaning. In "Thank You, M'am," many of the facts are very close to what we see in our daily lives, but this won't be the case in every story.

Many times a leader will ask a factual question in order to get you to back up your idea with evidence from the story. Suppose someone says, "Mrs. Jones is a little harsh because she has a tough job." The leader might then ask, "Where does Mrs. Jones work?" A question like this has only one correct answer, which can be given by pointing to the place in the story that reads "Instead, as they ate, she told him about her job in a hotel beauty shop that stayed open late . . ."

Occasionally you will be asked a factual question that cannot be answered by looking at any one passage. For example, the question "Does Mrs. Jones like Roger?" can only be answered yes. Although the story does not come right out and say so, Mrs. Jones' kindness shows that she does, and there is no evidence for any other answer.

Questions of interpretation occupy the central place in a Junior Great Books discussion. These are the questions that ask you to look carefully at what happens in a story and to consider what the story means. Unlike factual questions, they usually have more than one correct answer. Some interpretive questions focus on a specific passage or ask about a single event. For example, "Why does Roger answer truthfully when Mrs. Jones asks whether he will run away if she turns him loose?" One answer is that he's naturally an honest boy. Another is that he's trying to make Mrs. Jones believe he is truthful so that she will treat him less harshly.

Although questions about details are important, a leader will generally open discussion with an interpretive question that asks you to think about one of the main ideas in the story. An interpretive question opening a discussion of "Thank You, M'am" might be "Why do Mrs. Jones and Roger need each other?" When we are first introduced to Roger and Mrs. Jones, they seem to be characters without much in common. On looking more closely, however, we see that both are people without close families, both have gone through some hard times, and that Mrs. Jones has experience and knowledge she wants to share with

Roger. Each of these observations will help you decide how to begin answering this question.

Questions of evaluation ask whether you agree with what you have read and how the story fits with your own experience. As you read "Thank You, M'am," you might wonder, "Should Mrs. Jones have sent Roger away with a gift?" or "Would I have run when Mrs. Jones' back was turned?" As you try to answer these questions, you will have more to say about what you believe than about the story itself.

Since interpreting literature is the main purpose of the Junior Great Books program, you will spend most of your discussion time answering questions of interpretation. Questions of fact will help you support your opinions about what a story means. Questions of evaluation are interesting only after you have thought carefully about a story's meaning. ■

Fables

Leo Tolstoy

The King and the Shirt

A king once fell ill.

"I will give half my kingdom to the man who can cure me," he said.

All his wise men gathered together to decide how the king could be cured. But no one knew. Only one of the wise men said what he thought would cure the king.

"If you can find a happy man, take his shirt, put it on the king—and the king will be cured."

The king sent his emissaries to search for a happy man. They traveled far and wide throughout his whole kingdom, but they could not find a happy man. There was no one who was completely satisfied: if a man was rich he was ailing; if he was healthy he was poor; if he was rich and healthy he had a bad wife; or if he had children they were bad—everyone had something to complain of.

Finally, late one night, the king's son was passing by a poor little hut and he heard someone say:

"Now, God be praised, I have finished my work, I have eaten my fill, and I can lie down and sleep! What more could I want?"

The king's son rejoiced and gave orders that the man's shirt be taken and carried to the king, and that the man be given as much money as he wanted.

The emissaries went in to take off the man's shirt, but the happy man was so poor that he had no shirt.

Interpretive Questions

1. Is the happy man content because he wants so little or because he has so little?

2. Why does it turn out that the happy man has no shirt?

3. According to the story, must one be poor in order to be happy?

The Two Brothers

Two brothers set out on a journey together. At noon they lay down in a forest to rest. When they woke up they saw a stone lying next to them. There was something written on the stone, and they tried to make out what it was.

"Whoever finds this stone," they read, "let him go straight into the forest at sunrise. In the forest a river will appear; let him swim across the river to the other side. There he will find a she-bear and her cubs. Let him take the cubs from her and run up the mountain with them, without once looking back. On top of the mountain he will see a house, and in that house he will find happiness."

When they had read what was written on the stone, the younger brother said:

"Let us go together. We can swim across the river, carry off the bear cubs, take them to the house on the mountain, and together find happiness."

"I am not going into the forest after bear cubs," said the elder brother, "and I advise you not to go. In the first place, no one can know whether what is written on this stone is the truth—perhaps it was written in jest. It is even possible that we have not read it correctly. In the second place, even if what is written here is the truth—suppose we go into the forest and night comes, and we cannot find the river. We shall be lost. And if we do find the river, how are we going to swim across it? It may be broad and swift. In the third place, even if we swim across the river, do you think it is an easy thing to take her cubs away from a she-bear? She will seize us, and instead of finding happiness, we shall perish, and all for nothing. In the fourth place, even if we succeeded in carrying off the bear cubs, we could not run up a mountain without stopping to rest. And, most important of all, the stone does not tell us what kind of happiness we should find in that house. It may be that happiness awaiting us there is not at all the sort of happiness we would want."

"In my opinion," said the younger brother, "you are wrong. What is written on the stone could not have been put there without reason. And it is all perfectly clear. In the first place, no harm will come to us if we try. In the second place, if we do not go, someone else will read the inscription on the stone and find happiness, and we shall have lost it all. In the third place, if you do not make an effort and try hard, nothing in the world will succeed. In the fourth place, I should not want it thought that I was afraid of anything."

The elder brother answered him by saying: "The proverb says: 'In seeking great happiness small pleasures may be lost.' And also: 'A bird in the hand is worth two in the bush.' "

The younger brother replied: "I have heard: 'He who is afraid of the leaves must not go into the forest.' And also: 'Beneath a stone no water flows.' "

Then the younger brother set off, and the elder remained behind.

No sooner had the younger brother gone into the forest than he found the river, swam across it, and there on the other side was the she-bear, fast asleep. He took her cubs, and ran up the mountain without looking back. When he reached the top of the mountain the people came out to meet him with a carriage to take him into the city, where they made him their king.

He ruled for five years. In the sixth year, another king, who was stronger than he, waged war against him. The city was conquered, and he was driven out.

Again the younger brother became a wanderer, and he arrived one day at the house of the elder brother. The elder brother was living in a village and had grown neither rich nor poor. The two brothers rejoiced at seeing each other and at once began telling of all that had happened to them.

"You see," said the elder brother, "I was right. Here I have lived quietly and well, while you, though you may have been a king, have seen a great deal of trouble."

"I do not regret having gone into the forest and up the mountain," replied the younger brother. "I may have nothing now, but I shall always have something to remember, while you have no memories at all."

Interpretive Questions

1. Are we supposed to think that one brother made a better choice than the other?
2. Why is each brother satisfied with his own life?
3. Does the writing on the stone tell the truth?

The Rules of Discussion

These four rules guide Junior Great Books discussions. Following them makes it easier for leaders and students to help one another understand and appreciate stories. Show them to your parents when you describe what happens in a discussion.

1. **No one may take part in the discussion without first reading the story.** If you haven't read the story, you can't help others understand its meaning. It is also very confusing to hear opinions that don't come from firsthand knowledge of the story.
2. **Discuss only the story everyone has read.** This rule gives everyone an equal chance to contribute. It makes sure that discussion will only be about a story everyone knows.
3. **Do not introduce other people's opinions unless you can back them up with evidence from the story.** When you take another person's word for what the story means, you are no longer thinking for yourself. This rule does not mean you may not use an idea you hear from someone else. But make sure you understand the idea and can support it with evidence from the story, just as if you had thought it up yourself.
4. **Leaders may only ask questions. They may not answer them.** Leaders never offer their own opinions. Instead, they share their questions about the story's meaning. By responding to the leader's questions and your classmates' answers, you help the group—including the leader—reach a better understanding of the story. ■

The Happy Prince

Oscar Wilde

High above the city, on a tall column, stood the statue of the Happy Prince. He was gilded all over with thin leaves of fine gold, for eyes he had two bright sapphires, and a large red ruby glowed on his sword hilt.

"He was very much admired indeed. He is as beautiful as a weathercock," remarked one of the Town Councillors who wished to gain a reputation for having artistic tastes. "Only not quite so useful," he added, fearing lest people should think him unpractical, which he really was not.

"Why can't you be like the Happy Prince?" asked a sensible mother of her little boy, who was crying for the moon. "The Happy Prince never dreams of crying for anything."

"I am glad there is someone in the world who is quite happy," muttered a disappointed man as he gazed at the wonderful statue.

"He looks just like an angel," said the Charity Children as they came out of the cathedral in their bright scarlet cloaks and their clean white pinafores.

"How do you know?" said the Mathematical Master. "You have never seen one."

"Ah! but we have, in our dreams," answered the children; and the Mathematical Master frowned and looked very severe, for he did not approve of children dreaming.

One night there flew over the city a little Swallow. His friends had gone away to Egypt six weeks before, but he had stayed behind, for he was in love with the most beautiful Reed. He had met her early in the spring as he was flying down the river after a big yellow moth, and had been so attracted by her slender waist that he had stopped to talk to her.

"Shall I love you?" said the Swallow, who liked to come to the point at once, and the Reed made him a low bow. So he flew round and round her, touching the water with his wings, and making silver ripples. This was his courtship, and it lasted all through the summer.

"It is a ridiculous attachment," twittered the other Swallows. "She has no money, and far too many relations." And indeed the river was quite full of Reeds. Then, when the autumn came they all flew away.

After they had gone he felt lonely and began to tire of his lady-love. "She has no conversation," he said, "and

I am afraid that she is a coquette, for she is always flirting with the wind." And certainly, whenever the wind blew, the Reed made the most graceful curtsies. "I admit that she is domestic," he continued, "but I love travelling, and my wife, consequently, should love travelling also."

"Will you come away with me?" he said finally to her, but the Reed shook her head, she was so attached to her home.

"You have been trifling with me," he cried. "I am off to the Pyramids. Goodbye!" and he flew away.

All day long he flew, and at nighttime he arrived at the city. "Where shall I put up?" he said. "I hope the town has made preparations."

Then he saw the statue on the tall column.

"I will put up there," he cried. "It is a fine position, with plenty of fresh air." So he alighted just between the feet of the Happy Prince.

"I have a golden bedroom," he said softly to himself as he looked round, and he prepared to go to sleep; but just as he was putting his head under his wing a large drop of water fell on him. "What a curious thing!" he cried. "There is not a single cloud in the sky, the stars are quite clear and bright, and yet it is raining. The climate in the north of Europe is really dreadful. The Reed used to like the rain, but that was merely her selfishness."

Then another drop fell.

"What is the use of a statue if it cannot keep the rain off?" he said. "I must look for a good chimney pot." And he determined to fly away.

But before he had opened his wings, a third drop fell, and he looked up, and saw—Ah! what did he see?

The eyes of the Happy Prince were filled with tears, and tears were running down his golden cheeks. His face was so beautiful in the moonlight that the little Swallow was filled with pity.

"Who are you?" he said.

"I am the Happy Prince."

"Why are you weeping then?" asked the Swallow. "You have quite drenched me."

"When I was alive and had a human heart," answered the statue, "I did not know what tears were, for I lived in the Palace of Sans-Souci, where sorrow is not allowed to enter. In the daytime I played with my companions in the garden, and in the evening I led the dance in the Great Hall. Round the garden ran a very lofty wall, but I never cared to ask what lay beyond it, everything about me was so beautiful. My courtiers called me the Happy Prince, and happy indeed I was, if pleasure be happiness. So I lived, and so I died. And now that I am dead they have set me up here so high that I can see all the ugliness and all the misery of my city, and though my heart is made of lead yet I cannot choose but weep."

"What! is he not solid gold?" said the Swallow to himself. He was too polite to make any personal remarks out loud.

"Far away," continued the statue in a low musical voice, "far away in a little street there is a poor house. One of the windows is open, and through it I can see a woman seated at a table. Her face is thin and worn, and she has coarse, red hands, all pricked by the needle, for she is a seamstress. She is embroidering passionflowers on a satin gown for the loveliest of the Queen's maids of honor to wear at the next Court ball. In a bed in the corner of the room her little boy is lying ill. He has a fever and is asking for oranges. His mother has nothing to give him but river water, so he is crying. Swallow, Swallow, little Swallow, will you not bring her the ruby out of my sword hilt? My feet are fastened to this pedestal and I cannot move."

"I am waited for in Egypt," said the Swallow. "My friends are flying up and down the Nile and talking to the large lotus flowers. Soon they will go to sleep in the tomb of the great King. The King is there himself in his painted coffin. He is wrapped in yellow linen and embalmed with spices. Round his neck is a chain of pale green jade, and his hands are like withered leaves."

"Swallow, Swallow, little Swallow," said the Prince, "will you not stay with me for one night and be my messenger? The boy is so thirsty and the mother so sad."

"I don't think I like boys," answered the Swallow. "Last summer, when I was staying on the river, there were two rude boys, the miller's sons, who were always throwing stones at me. They never hit me, of course. We swallows fly far too well for that, and besides I come of a family famous for its agility; but still, it was a mark of disrespect."

But the Happy Prince looked so sad that the little

Swallow was sorry. "It is very cold here," he said, "but I will stay with you for one night and be your messenger."

"Thank you, little Swallow," said the Prince.

So the Swallow picked out the great ruby from the Prince's sword and flew away with it in his beak over the roofs of the town.

He passed by the cathedral tower, where the white marble angels were sculptured. He passed by the palace and heard the sound of dancing. A beautiful girl came out on the balcony with her lover. "How wonderful the stars are," he said to her, "and how wonderful is the power of love!"

"I hope my dress will be ready in time for the State ball," she answered. "I have ordered passionflowers to be embroidered on it, but the seamstresses are so lazy."

He passed over the river and saw the lanterns hanging to the masts of the ships. He passed over the Ghetto and saw the old Jews bargaining with each other and weighing out money in copper scales. At last he came to the poor house and looked in. The boy was tossing feverishly on his bed, and the mother had fallen asleep, she was so tired. In he hopped, and laid the great ruby on the table beside the woman's thimble. Then he flew gently round the bed, fanning the boy's forehead with his wings. "How cool I feel!" said the boy. "I must be getting better." And he sank into a delicious slumber.

Then the Swallow flew back to the Happy Prince and told him what he had done. "It is curious," he remarked, "but I feel quite warm now, although it is so cold."

"That is because you have done a good action." said the Prince. And the little Swallow began to think, and then he fell asleep. Thinking always made him sleepy.

When day broke he flew down the river and had a bath. "What a remarkable phenomenon!" said the Professor of Ornithology as he was passing over the bridge. "A swallow in winter!" And he wrote a long letter about it to the local newspaper. Everyone quoted it, it was full of so many words that they could not understand.

"Tonight I go to Egypt," said the Swallow, and he was in high spirits at the prospect. He visited all the public monuments and sat a long time on the top of the church steeple. Wherever he went the Sparrows chirruped and said to each other. "What a distinguished stranger!" So he enjoyed himself very much.

When the moon rose he flew back to the Happy Prince. "Have you any commissions for Egypt?" he cried. "I am just starting."

"Swallow, Swallow, little Swallow," said the Prince, "will you not stay with me one night longer?"

"I am waited for in Egypt," answered the Swallow. "Tomorrow my friends will fly up to the Second Cataract. The river horse couches there among the bulrushes, and on a great granite throne sits the God Memnon. All night long he watches the stars, and when the morning star shines he utters one cry of joy, and then he is silent. At noon the yellow lions come down to the water's edge to drink. They have eyes like green beryls, and their roar is louder than the roar of the cataract."

"Swallow, Swallow, little Swallow," said the Prince, "far away across the city I see a young man in a garret. He is leaning over a desk covered with papers, and in a tumbler by his side there is a bunch of withered violets. His hair is brown and crisp, and his lips are red as a pomegranate, and he has large and dreamy eyes. He is trying to finish a play for the Director of the Theater, but he is too cold to write any more. There is no fire in the grate, and hunger has made him faint."

"I will wait with you one night longer," said the Swallow, who really had a good heart. "Shall I take him another ruby?"

"Alas! I have no ruby now," said the Prince. "My eyes are all that I have left. They are made of rare sapphires, which were brought out of India a thousand years ago. Pluck out one of them and take it to him. He will sell it to the jeweller, and buy firewood, and finish his play."

"Dear Prince," said the Swallow, "I cannot do that." And he began to weep.

"Swallow, Swallow, little Swallow," said the Prince, "do as I command you."

So the Swallow plucked out the Prince's eye and flew away to the student's garret. It was easy enough to get in, as there was a hole in the roof. Through this he darted, and came into the room. The young man had his head buried in his hands, so he did not hear the flutter of the bird's wings, and when he looked up he found the beautiful sapphire lying on the withered violets.

"I am beginning to be appreciated," he cried. "This is

from some great admirer. Now I can finish my play." And he looked quite happy.

The next day the Swallow flew down to the harbor. He sat on the mast of a large vessel and watched the sailors hauling big chests out of the hold with ropes. "Heave a-hoy!" they shouted as each chest came up. "I am going to Egypt!" cried the Swallow, but nobody minded, and when the moon rose he flew back to the Happy Prince.

"I am come to bid you goodbye," he cried.

"Swallow, Swallow, little Swallow," said the Prince, "will you not stay with me one night longer?"

"It is winter," answered the Swallow, "and the chill snow will soon be here. In Egypt the sun is warm on the green palm trees, and the crocodiles lie in the mud and look lazily about them. My companions are building a nest in the Temple of Baalbek, and the pink and white doves are watching them and cooing to each other. Dear Prince, I must leave you, but I will never forget you, and next spring I will bring you back two beautiful jewels in place of those you have given away. The ruby shall be redder than a red rose, and the sapphire shall be as blue as the great sea."

"In the square below," said the Happy Prince, "there stands a little match-girl. She has let her matches fall in the gutter, and they are all spoiled. Her father will beat her if she does not bring home some money, and she is crying. She has no shoes or stockings, and her little head is bare. Pluck out my other eye, and give it to her, and her father will not beat her."

"I will stay with you one night longer," said the Swallow, "but I cannot pluck out your eye. You would be quite blind then."

"Swallow, Swallow, little Swallow," said the Prince, "do as I command you."

So he plucked out the Prince's other eye, and darted down with it. He swooped past the match-girl and slipped the jewel into the palm of her hand. "What a lovely bit of glass!" cried the little girl, and she ran home laughing.

Then the Swallow came back to the Prince. "You are blind now," he said, "so I will stay with you always."

"No, little Swallow," said the poor Prince, "you must go away to Egypt."

"I will stay with you always," said the Swallow, and he slept at the Prince's feet.

All the next day he sat on the Prince's shoulder and told him stories of what he had seen in strange lands. He told him of the red ibises, who stand in long rows on the banks of the Nile and catch goldfish in their beaks; of the Sphinx, who is as old as the world itself, and lives in the desert, and knows everything; of the merchants, who walk slowly by the side of their camels and carry amber beads in their hands; of the King of the Mountains of the Moon, who is as black as ebony and worships a large crystal; of the great green snake that sleeps in a palm tree, and has twenty priests to feed it with honey cakes; and of the pygmies who sail over a big lake on large flat leaves and are always at war with the butterflies.

"Dear little Swallow," said the Prince, "you tell me of

marvelous things, but more marvelous than anything is the suffering of men and of women. There is no Mystery so great as Misery. Fly over my city, little Swallow, and tell me what you see there."

So the Swallow flew over the great city, and saw the rich making merry in their beautiful houses, while the beggars were sitting at the gates. He flew into dark lanes, and saw the white faces of starving children looking out listlessly at the black streets. Under the archway of a bridge two little boys were lying in one another's arms to try and keep themselves warm. "How hungry we are!" they said. "You must not lie here," shouted the watchman, and they wandered out into the rain.

Then he flew back and told the Prince what he had seen.

"I am covered with fine gold," said the Prince. "You must take it off, leaf by leaf, and give it to my poor; the living always think that gold can make them happy."

Leaf after leaf of the fine gold the Swallow picked off, till the Happy Prince looked quite dull and gray. Leaf after leaf of the fine gold he brought to the poor, and the children's faces grew rosier, and they laughed and played games in the street. "We have bread now!" they cried.

Then the snow came, and after the snow came the frost. The streets looked as if they were made of silver, they were so bright and glistening; long icicles like crystal daggers hung down from the eaves of the houses, everybody went about in furs, and the little boys wore scarlet caps and skated on the ice.

The poor little Swallow grew colder and colder, but he would not leave the Prince, he loved him too well. He picked up crumbs outside the baker's door when the baker was not looking, and tried to keep himself warm by flapping his wings.

But at last he knew that he was going to die. He had just enough strength to fly up to the Prince's shoulder once more. "Goodbye, dear Prince!" he murmured. "Will you let me kiss your hand?"

"I am glad that you are going to Egypt at last, little Swallow," said the Prince. "You have stayed too long here; but you must kiss me on the lips, for I love you."

"It is not to Egypt that I am going," said the Swallow. "I am going to the House of Death. Death is the brother of Sleep, is he not?"

And he kissed the Happy Prince on the lips, and fell down dead at his feet.

At that moment a curious crack sounded inside the statue, as if something had broken. The fact is that the leaden heart had snapped right in two. It certainly was a dreadfully hard frost.

Early the next morning the Mayor was walking in the square below in company with the Town Councillors. As they passed the column he looked up at the statue. "Dear me! How shabby the Happy Prince looks!" he said.

"How shabby, indeed!" cried the Town Councillors, who always agreed with the Mayor, and they went up to look at it.

"The ruby has fallen out of his sword, his eyes are

gone, and he is golden no longer," said the Mayor. "In fact, he is little better than a beggar!"

"Little better than a beggar," said the Town Councillors.

"And here is actually a dead bird at his feet!" continued the Mayor. "We must really issue a proclamation that birds are not to be allowed to die here." And the Town Clerk made a note of the suggestion.

So they pulled down the statue of the Happy Prince. "As he is no longer beautiful he is no longer useful," said the Art Professor at the University.

Then they melted the statue in a furnace, and the Mayor held a meeting of the Corporation to decide what was to be done with the metal. "We must have another statue, of course," he said, "and it shall be a statue of myself."

"Of myself," said each of the Town Councillors, and they quarrelled. When I last heard of them they were quarrelling still.

"What a strange thing!" said the overseer of the workmen at the foundry. "This broken lead heart will not melt in the furnace. We must throw it away." So they threw it on a dustheap where the dead Swallow was also lying.

"Bring me the two most precious things in the city," said God to one of His Angels; and the Angel brought Him the leaden heart and the dead bird.

"You have rightly chosen," said God, "for in my garden of Paradise this little bird shall sing for evermore, and in my city of gold the Happy Prince shall praise me."

Interpretive Questions

1. Does the Prince believe people can be happy? Does he think they should be happy?
2. Is the Prince selfish to ask the Swallow to stay on night after night, even though the winter is dangerous for him?
3. Why is the Prince made to lose his beauty doing good deeds?

PRACTICE

Questions of Fact, Interpretation, and Evaluation

"The Happy Prince"

This exercise will give you practice in recognizing the differences between the three kinds of questions asked in a Junior Great Books discussion. In the blank before each of the following questions, write (F) if the question is FACTUAL, (I) if it is INTERPRETIVE, or (E) if it is EVALUATIVE. Reread the essay called "Questions of Fact, Interpretation, and Evaluation" before you begin.

____ 1. Why does the Swallow leave for Egypt six weeks late?

____ 2. Why does the Prince give gold to the poor even though he doesn't think it can make them happy?

____ 3. Can money make people happy?

____ 4. Why does the Swallow think it is raining when he first lands in the city?

____ 5. Why is the Swallow shown to be vain and silly in his romance with the Reed?

____ 6. Why does the author have the Swallow and the Happy Prince rewarded for their kind deeds only in Paradise?

____ 7. Why is the Happy Prince unhappy?

____ 8. Are rich people responsible for helping the poor?

____ 9. Why is the statue of the Happy Prince pulled down?

____ 10. Do you think the Prince should have asked the Swallow to risk his life in order to help the poor?

Fresh

Philippa Pearce

The force of water through the river gates scoured to a deep bottom; then the river shallowed again. People said the pool below the gates was very deep. Deep enough to drown in anyway.

At the bottom of the pool lived the freshwater mussels. No one had seen them there—most people would not have been particularly interested in them anyway. But if you were poking about among the stones in the shallows below the pool, you couldn't help finding mussel shells occasionally. Sometimes one by itself; sometimes two still hinged together. Gray-blue or green-gray on the outside; on the inside, a faint sheen of mother-of-pearl.

The Webster boys were fishing with their nets in the shallows for minnows, freshwater shrimps—anything that moved—when they found a freshwater mussel that was not just a pair of empty shells.

Dan Webster found it. He said: "Do you want this shell? It's double." While Laurie Webster was saying, "Let's see," Dan was lifting it and had noticed that the two shells were clamped together and that they had unusual weight. "They're not empty shells," he said. "They've something inside. It's alive."

He stooped again to hold the mussel in the palm of his hand so that the river water washed over it. Water creatures prefer water.

Laurie had splashed over to him. Now he crouched with the river lapping near the tops of his Wellington boots. "A freshwater mussel!" he said. "I've never owned one." He put out fingers to touch it—perhaps to take it—as it lay on the watery palm of Dan's hand. Dan's fingers curled up into a protective wall. "Careful," he said.

Together, as they were now, the Webster boys looked like brothers, but they were cousins. Laurie was the visitor. He lived in London and had an aquarium on his bedroom windowsill, instead of a river almost at his back door as Dan had. Dan was older than Laurie; Laurie admired Dan, and Dan was kind to Laurie. They did things together. Dan helped Laurie to find livestock for his aquarium—shrimps, leeches, flatworms, water snails variously whorled; whatever the turned stone and stooping net might bring them. During a visit by Laurie, they would fish often, but—until the last day—without a jam jar, just for the fun of it. On the last day, they took a jam jar and put their more interesting catches into it for Laurie's journey back to London.

Now they had found a freshwater mussel on the second day of Laurie's visit. Five more days still to go.

"We can't keep it," said Dan. "Even if we got the jam jar, it couldn't live in a jam jar for five days. It would be dead by the time you got it back to the aquarium."

Laurie, who was quite young, looked as if he might cry. "I've never had the chance of a freshwater mussel before."

"Well . . . ," said Dan. He made as if to put it down among the stones and mud where he had found it.

"Don't! Don't! It's my freshwater mussel! Don't let it go!"

"And don't shout in my ear!" Dan said crossly. "Who said I was letting it go? I was just trying it out in the river again, to see whether it was safe to leave it there. I don't think the current would carry it away."

He put the mussel down in the shelter of a large, slimy stone. The current, breaking on the stone, flowed past without stirring it. But the mussel began to feel at home again. They could almost see it settling contentedly into the mud. After a while it parted the lips of its shells slightly, and a pastrylike substance crowded out a little way.

"What's it *doing?* " whispered Laurie. But this was not the sort of thing that Dan knew, and Laurie would not find out until he got back to his aquarium books in London.

Now they saw that they had not merely imagined the mussel to be settling in. There was less of it visible out of the mud—much less of it.

"It's burying itself. It's escaping," said Laurie. "Don't let it!"

Dan sighed and took the mussel back into the palm of his hand again. The mussel, disappointed, shut up tight.

"We need to keep it in the river," said Dan, "but somewhere where it can't escape."

They looked around. They weren't sure what they were looking for, and at first they certainly weren't finding it.

Still with the mussel in his hand, Dan turned to the banks. They were overhanging, with river water swirling against them and under them. The roots of trees and bushes made a kind of very irregular lattice fencing through which the water ran continually.

"I wonder . . . ," said Dan.

"You couldn't keep it there," Laurie said. "It'd be child's play for a freshwater mussel to escape through the roots."

Dan stared at the roots. "I've a better idea," he said. "I'll stay here with the mussel. You go back to our house—to the larder. You'll find a little white plastic carton with Eileen's slimming cress* growing in it." Eileen was Dan's elder sister, whose absorbing interest was her figure. "Empty the cress out onto a plate—I'll square Eileen later. Bring the plastic carton back here."

Laurie never questioned Dan. He set off across the meadows towards the house.

---

* *cress.* A plant whose leaves can be eaten in salads.

Dan and the freshwater mussel were left alone to wait.

Dan was holding the freshwater mussel as he had done before, stooping down to the river with his hand in the water. It occurred to him to repeat the experiment that Laurie had interrupted. He put the mussel down in the lee of the slimy stone again and watched. Again the current left the mussel undisturbed. Again the mussel began to settle itself into the mud between the stones.

Down—gently down—down. . . . The freshwater mussel was now as deep in the mud as when Laurie had called out in fear of losing it; but now Laurie was not there. Dan did not interfere. He simply watched the mussel ease itself down—down. . . .

Soon less than a quarter of an inch of mussel shell was showing above the mud. The shell was nearly the same color as the mud embedding it: Dan could identify it only by keeping his eyes fixed continuously upon its projection. That lessened, until it had almost disappeared.

Entirely disappeared. . . .

Still Dan stared. As long as he kept his eyes on the spot where the mussel had disappeared, he could get it again. He had only to dig his fingers into the mud at that exact spot to find it. If he let his eyes stray, the mussel was lost forever; there were so many slimy stones like that one, and mud was everywhere. He must keep his eyes fixed on the spot.

"Dan—Dan—Dan!" Laurie's voice came over the meadows. "I've got it!"

He nearly shifted his stare from the spot by the nondescript stone. It would have been so natural to lift his head in response to the calling voice. He was tempted to do it. But he had to remember that this was Laurie's mussel, and it must not be lost; he did remember. He kept his gaze fixed and dug quickly with his fingers and got the mussel again.

There he was standing with the mussel in the palm of his hand, and water and mud dripping from it, when Laurie came in sight. "Is it all right?" he shouted.

"Yes," said Dan.

Laurie climbed down the riverbank into the water with the plastic carton in his hand. Dan looked at it and nodded. "It has holes in the bottom, and we can make some more along the sides with a penknife." He did so, while Laurie held the mussel.

"Now," Dan said, "put the mussel in the carton with some mud and little stones to make it comfortable. That's it. The next thing is to wedge the carton between the roots under the bank at just the right level, so that the water flows through the holes in the carton, without flowing over the whole thing. The mussel will have his flowing river, but he won't be able to escape."

Laurie said, "I wish I could think of things like that."

Dan tried fitting the plastic carton between the roots in several different places, until he found a grip that was just at the right height. Gently he tested the firmness of the wedging, and it held.

"Oh," said Laurie, "it's just perfect, Dan. Thank you.

I shall really get it back to the aquarium now. My first freshwater mussel. I shall call it—well, what would *you* call it, Dan?"

"Go on," said Dan. "It's your freshwater mussel. You name it."

"I shall call it Fresh then." Laurie leaned forward to see Fresh, already part buried in his mud, dim in the shadow of the bank, but absolutely a captive. He stood up again and moved back to admire the arrangement from a distance. Then he realized a weakness. "Oh, it'll never do. The plastic's so white. Anyone might notice it and come over to look, and tip Fresh out."

"We'll hide him then," said Dan. He found an old brick among the stones of the shallows and brought it over to the bank roots. He upended the brick in the water, leaning it in a casual pose against the roots, so that it concealed the white plastic carton altogether.

"There," he said.

Laurie sighed. "Really perfect."

"He should be safe there."

"For five days?"

"I tell you what," said Dan, "we could slip down here every day just to have a check on him. To make sure the level of the water through the carton isn't too high or hasn't sunk too low."

Laurie nodded. "Every day."

The daily visit to Fresh was a pleasure that Laurie looked forward to. On the third day it poured with rain, but they put on anoraks* as well as boots and made their check as usual. On the fourth day, they reached the river-bank to find a man fishing on the other side of the pool.

The fisherman was minding his own business and only gave them a sidelong glance as they came to a stop on the bank above Fresh's watery dungeon. (They knew its location exactly by now, even from across the meadow.) The man wasn't interested in them—yet. But if they clambered down into the river and began moving old bricks and poking about behind them, he would take notice. He would ask them what they were up to. When they had gone, he would perhaps come over and have a look for himself. He was wearing waders.

"Not now," Dan said quietly. "Later." And they turned away, as though they had come only to look at the view.

They went back after their tea, but the fisherman was still there. In the meantime, Laurie had worked himself into a desperation. "All that rain yesterday has made the river rise. It'll be washing Fresh out of the carton."

"No," said Dan. "You've just got Fresh on the brain. The river's hardly risen at all. If at all. Fresh is all right."

"Why can't that man go home?"

"He'll go home at dusk anyway," said Dan.

"That'll be too late for us. I shall be going to bed by then. You know your mum said I must."

"Yes." Dan looked at him thoughtfully. "Would you like *me* to come? I mean, Mum couldn't stop my being out that bit later than you, because I am that bit older."

---

* *anorak.* A hooded parka.

"Oh, would you—*would* you?" cried Laurie. "Oh, thanks, Dan."

"Oh, don't thank me," said Dan.

Everything went according to plan, except that Dan, getting down to the river just before dark, found the fisherman still there. But he was in the act of packing up. He did not see Dan. He packed up and walked away, whistling sadly to himself. When the whistling had died away, Dan got down into the river and moved the brick and took out the plastic container. It had been at a safe water level, in spite of the rains, and Fresh was inside, alive and well.

Dan took Fresh out of the carton just to make sure. Then he put him among the stones in the river for the fun of seeing his disappearing act. As he watched, Dan reflected that this was what Fresh would have done if the fisherman *had* spotted the carton and taken him out of it for a good look, and then by mistake dropped him into the water. The fisherman would have lost sight of him, and Fresh would have buried himself. He would have been gone for good—for good, back into the river.

The only signs would have been the brick moved, the plastic container out of place. And Fresh gone. That was all that Dan could have reported to Laurie.

But it had not happened, after all.

Dan picked up Fresh and put him back in the carton and put the carton back, and then the brick, and then walked home. He told Laurie, sitting in his pajamas in front of the TV with his supper, that everything had been all right. He did not say more.

On the fifth day, the day before Laurie's return to London, they went together to the riverbank. There was no fisherman. The brick was exactly in place and behind it the plastic carton, with the water flowing through correctly. There was Fresh, safe, sound, and apparently not even pining at captivity.

"Tomorrow," said Laurie. "Tomorrow morning we'll bring the jam jar, ready for me to take him home on the train."

That night was the last of Laurie's visit. He and Dan shared Dan's bedroom, and tonight they went to bed at the same time and fell asleep together.

Dan's father was the last person to go to bed at the end of the evening. He bolted the doors and turned out the last lights. That usually did not wake Dan, but tonight it did. Suddenly he was wide awake in the complete darkness, hearing the sound of his parents going to bed in their room, hearing the sound of Laurie's breathing in the next bed, the slow, whispering breath of deep sleep.

The movements and murmurs from the other bedroom ceased; Laurie's breathing continued evenly. Dan still lay wide awake.

He had never really noticed before how very dark everything could be. It was more than blackness; it seemed to fill space as water fills a pool. It seemed to fill the inside of his head.

He lay for some time with the darkness everywhere; then he got up very quietly. He put trousers and sweater on over his pajamas, bunchily. Laurie's breathing never changed. He tiptoed out of the bedroom and downstairs. In the hall, he put on his Wellington boots. He let himself out of the house and then through the front gate. There was no one about, no lights in the houses, except for a night light where a child slept. There was one lamp in the lane, and that sent his shadow leaping horribly ahead of him. Then he turned a corner and the lamplight had gone. He was taking the short cut towards the river.

No moon tonight. No stars. Darkness. . . .

He had been born here; he had always lived here; he knew these meadows as well as he knew himself; but the darkness made him afraid. He could not see the familiar way ahead; he had to remember it. He felt his way. He scented it. He smelled the river before he came to it, and he felt the vegetation changing underfoot, growing ranker when he reached the bank.

He lowered himself into the water, from darkness into darkness. He began to feel along the roots of the bank for the upended brick. He found it quickly—he had not been far out in the point at which he had struck the bank.

His hand was on the brick, and he kept it there while he tried to see. In the darkness and through the darkness, he tried to see what was going to happen—what he was going to make happen. What he was going to do.

Now that he was no longer moving, he could hear the sound of other movements in the darkness. He heard the water flowing. He heard a *drip* of water into water somewhere near him; a long pause; another *drip*. He heard a quick, quiet birdcall that was strange to him; certainly not an owl—he used to hear those as he lay snug in bed in his bedroom at home. And whatever sound he heard now, he heard beneath it the ceaseless, watery, whispering sound of the river, as if the river were alive and breathing in its sleep in the darkness, like Laurie left sleeping in the bedroom at home.

It was within his power to move the brick and take hold of the plastic carton and tip it right over. Fresh would fall into the water with a *plop* so tiny that he might never hear it above the flow of the river. In such darkness, there would be no question of finding Fresh again, ever.

If he meant to do it, he could do it in three seconds. His hand was on the brick.

But did he mean to do it?

He tried to see what was in his mind, but his mind was like a deep pool of darkness. He didn't know what he really meant to do.

Suddenly he took his hand from the brick and stood erect. He put his booted foot on one of the lateral roots that extended behind the brick. He had to feel for it with his toe. Having found it, he pressed it slowly downwards; then quickly took his foot off again. He could feel the root, released from the pressure, following his foot upwards again in a little jerk.

That jerk of the root might have been enough to upset or at least tilt the carton. It might have been enough to tip Fresh out into the river.

On the other hand, of course, it might not have been enough.

Dan flung himself at the bank well to one side of the brick and clambered up and began a blundering run across the meadows. He did not slow up or go more carefully until he reached the lamplight of the lane and the possibility of someone's hearing his footsteps.

He let himself into the house and secured the door behind him. He left his boots in the hall and his clothes on the chair in the bedroom. He crept back into bed. Laurie was still breathing gently and regularly.

Dan slept late the next morning. He woke to bright sunshine flooding the room and Laurie banging on the bedrail. "Fresh! Fresh! Fresh!" he was chanting. Dan looked at him through eyes half-shut. He was trying to remember a dream he had had last night. It had been a dream of darkness—too dark to remember, or to want to remember. But when he went downstairs to breakfast and saw his boots in the hall with mud still drying on them, he knew that he had not dreamed last night.

Immediately after breakfast, they went down to the river. Laurie was carrying his jam jar.

They climbed down into the shallows as usual. Laurie made a little sound of dismay when he saw the brick. "It's lopsided—the current's moved it!"

Dan stood at a distance in the shallows while Laurie scrabbled the brick down into the water with a splash. There behind it was the white plastic carton, but at a considerable tilt, so that water flowed steadily from its lowest corner. "Oh, Fresh—Fresh!" Laurie implored in a whisper. He was peering into the carton.

"Well?" said Dan, from his distance, not moving.

"Oh, no!" Laurie exclaimed, low but in dismay.

"Well?"

Laurie was poking with a finger at the bottom of the carton. Suddenly he laughed. "He's here after all! It's all right! It was just that burying trick of his! Fresh is here!"

Laurie was beaming.

Dan said, "I'm glad."

Laurie transferred Fresh from the carton to the jam jar, together with some mud and stones and a suitable amount of river water. Dan watched him.

Then they both set off across the meadows again, Laurie holding the jam jar carefully, as he would need to do—as he *would* do—during all the long journey to London. He was humming to himself. He stopped to say to Dan, "I say, I did thank you for Fresh, didn't I?"

"Don't thank me," said Dan.

Interpretive Questions

1. Why can't Dan decide whether to let the mussel go or keep it for Laurie?
2. Why does Dan leave it to chance whether or not Fresh falls back into the river?
3. Is Dan telling the truth when he tells Laurie he's glad Fresh hasn't escaped?

PRACTICE

Questions of Fact, Interpretation, and Evaluation

"Fresh"

Here is another exercise to give you practice in recognizing the differences between questions of fact, questions of interpretation, and questions of evaluation. Reread the essay called "Questions of Fact, Interpretation, and Evaluation." Then mark the following questions (F) if they are FACTUAL, (I) if they are INTERPRETIVE, or (E) if they are EVALUATIVE.

____ 1. At the end of the story, why does Dan tell Laurie not to thank him?

____ 2. Should Dan have let Fresh go?

____ 3. Who found Fresh?

____ 4. Is Dan eager for Laurie to take Fresh back to London?

____ 5. Why does Dan think at first that he dreamed about going to the river at night?

____ 6. Did Dan know the mussel was alive when he gave it to Laurie?

____ 7. Is it right to remove a living creature from its natural environment?

____ 8. Why does the author have Dan's trip to the river take place on a very dark night?

____ 9. Why don't Laurie and Dan put the mussel in the jam jar right away?

____ 10. Why are we told that most people are not interested in freshwater mussels?